MW01122259

Getti

WITH
JAZZ
BAND

Lissa A. Fleming

The National Association for Music Education

Contents

Preface

A good instrumental music program is multifaceted and provides a solid foundation in performance through a variety of experiences. With the concert band as the central focus of the program, experiences in solo and chamber playing, jazz band, marching band, and pep band add variety and challenge to the instrumental music program.

Whether you are adding jazz band to your instrumental program or maintaining an existing jazz program, there are several important questions to be asked. *Why* offer jazz band? *What* should be the focus? *Who* should participate? *When* should the jazz band meet? There are no specific answers to these questions, rather, they must be considered with regard to the total music program at your particular school.

As you approach this new experience, you may be excited and, perhaps, feel some anxiety at the same time. This book, like all the books in the *Getting Started* series, is designed to help you get started. It may not answer every question or cover every contingency, but it does provide an outline to follow that may help build your confidence as you take on the new responsibilities associated with directing a jazz band.

Chapter 1

You're Teaching Jazz Band

Why Offer Jazz Band?

Jazz is a uniquely American art form that has a rich history and tradition. Because of the variety of styles and the opportunity for individual creative expression, jazz provides an outlet for more advanced students to develop technically, musically, and creatively. The jazz band is also a mobile and popular ensemble that can serve as a public relations vehicle for your music department and school.

A word of caution is needed. Your vision for the total music program must keep the education of every student as the primary goal. Constant performance demands from the school and community should not be allowed to interfere with the educational process. Performance should be an outcome of the learning that has taken place, not an end in itself. The jazz band must be kept in perspective with the total program—don't allow the jazz band to become the "tail that wags the dog."

What Should be the Focus?

Standard jazz repertoire with an emphasis on swing style should be the main emphasis. Historically important literature should be performed, and students should be exposed to contemporary styles including rock, funk, Latin, and fusion. Jazz band should also provide the opportunity for individual musical growth and creative expression. Improvisation is central to jazz. The development of aural skills and some knowledge of jazz theory pave the way for successful improvisation.

Who Should Participate?

Ideally, any student who has mastered the basics of playing his or her instrument should have the opportunity to participate in jazz band. Students in the jazz band are generally expected to be members of the concert band, as the jazz band is meant to supplement the concert band experience, not replace it.

If possible, there should be two jazz bands. One should be open to any interested student who can demonstrate solid fundamental playing, and the other should be selected by audition with only one student assigned to a part. One of the unique things about big band jazz is the sonority of the band achieved with only one player per part. The challenge to the student to be solely responsible for his or her part, as well as for the integrity to the art form, are strong arguments for making the top band a select group with proper instrumentation.

If there are not enough students to offer a second band, there are other options to consider. For example, a series of jazz "master classes" might be offered several times throughout the year to meet the needs of the students who do not make it into the band. Or, all interested students might be accepted into the band, with students sitting out on a tune when necessary to maintain one player per part. Everyone could play when sight reading and during early rehearsals of tunes, doubling parts where necessary.

When Should Jazz Band Meet?

There are advantages to having jazz band as a part of the curriculum, meeting during the school day. Students can be held accountable for attendance and class work and can receive a grade and academic credit. Having students daily for a forty- to fifty-minute class period also allows more time to teach jazz history, theory, and improvisation. The primary disadvantages to this configuration are that students do not have time in their already busy academic schedules or they encounter schedule conflicts. If students are required to be enrolled in concert band in order to participate in jazz band, then scheduling two periods of band each year becomes virtually impossible.

Meeting with the jazz band on an extracurricular basis is more workable in some situations. Finding a time that is clear of other extracurricular activities can be a problem. You must establish an attendance policy, decide what conflicts will be excused, and be firm and consistent with enforcement if the extracurricular jazz band is to be a success. Working with coaches and sponsors of other activities and refraining from scheduling performances and rehearsals at the last minute will help keep students from being placed in awkward situations.

An extracurricular jazz band is often faced with very limited rehearsal time. It is important to keep the number of performances in line with the time available for rehearsal. Development of aural skills, jazz theory, and improvisation as well as critical listening to jazz are extremely important to the success of the band. It is easy to overlook these components when faced with performance demands and find yourself only rehearsing music, not teaching students.

There are many other configurations that might fit your situation. One alternative is to offer an academic class in jazz improvisation at least one semester each year. Students could take this course once along with concert band. Jazz band then could be offered on an extracurricular basis. Another option is to have jazz band before or after the regular school day with students receiving academic credit and a grade for the course. This eliminates the problems of attendance and accountability of students in an extracurricular situation.

Getting Started

As you begin your job as a new band director, it is important to have a clear idea of your goals for the program and to establish fair policies that you can enforce. It is probably not a good idea to try to make a lot of changes immediately. You will want to talk to your principal, other teachers, students, and parents to find out how things have been done in the past. Objectively evaluate what has worked well and what areas are priorities for change. Identify areas for change that will not cost a lot of money or create controversy and begin working on these. As you become established in your position and gain the respect of administrators, students, and community members, you can work on the more costly and controversial changes.

Establishing Yourself in the School and Community

Communication is extremely important. Every time you contact administrators, students, and parents, you must clearly communicate your philosophy as director of the jazz band program.

Establishing a good relationship with the administration is vital to your success as a band director:

- Be sure that your principal is kept informed about your goals for the band program.
- Take time to keep him or her informed about your plans and activities before they happen.
- Do not make major decisions without asking for approval.
- Become fully acquainted with proper procedures and follow them carefully.
- If funds are available, mail a newsletter to parents several times a year with information about rehearsals, concerts, grading policy, and your plans for the band program. If this is not practical, find out if there is a school newsletter that could include your important information. Other options are to send newsletters home with students or pass out detailed information at parents' night or at a Parent Teachers Association meeting. Do not hesitate to call parents to ask for help with a project or to talk about their child's progress.

Sample Lesson Plan for First Rehearsal

45 Minutes

3:00–3:08	Warm up and tune (see Chapter 4 for suggestions).
3:08–3:12	Discuss syllabus, schedule, and rules.
3:12–3:17	Sight read *Now is the Time.*
3:17–3:27	Work on notes, rhythm, style, balance, and blend of short section of *Now is the Time* to give students a taste of your musical expectations.
3:27–3:32	Play recording of *St. Thomas.*
3:32–3:37	Sight read first half of *St. Thomas.*
3:37–3:45	Work on eight to sixteen measures of the full-band section of *St. Thomas.* Finish with a run-through of this section. Give students practice suggestions to prepare for the next rehearsal.

First Rehearsal

Your first rehearsal with the jazz band is extremely important. Whether you are meeting a newly formed jazz band or conducting your first rehearsal with an existing ensemble, the initial rehearsal is critical. Perhaps the most important factor is your selection of music. Not only will your choice of music give the students an idea of who you are and what you like, it will also let them know your assessment of their potential and your expectations.

Choose two or three tunes for the first rehearsal that will motivate and challenge your ensemble without overwhelming them. The selections should be of contrasting styles and range from moderately easy to moderately difficult. Remember, students will have immediate impressions about you and the upcoming year based on the experience that they have in the first rehearsal, so careful thought should go into the selection of music. If you are meeting an established band for the first time, you should research past programs and recordings of the band to see what music the band has typically performed in order to help you select music at an appropriate level. Play a quality professional recording of at least one of the tunes that you select so that the students will have a vision of your goals for the band.

Keep organizational details to a minimum—the band will be anxious to play. Give students a written copy of the syllabus, schedule, and rules, and discuss only the most critical points. Prepare music folios with the music and handouts prior to rehearsal, and place the folders on the students' stands. A short positive statement of your expectations about rehearsal atmosphere should set the tone. Remind students of your expectations if they are not met. It is important to establish a good working atmosphere from the beginning.

Plan your first rehearsal carefully, using a written lesson plan with estimates of the time each activity will take. Always plan more than you think you will need, but time your rehearsal so that it ends in a positive manner. Students should leave motivated to practice and anxious to attend the next rehearsal. Chapter 4 contains detailed suggestions for successful rehearsals with the jazz band.

Grading Policy

It is important to establish a grading policy and evaluate student progress frequently. Even if your jazz band is extracurricular, it is a good idea to establish some kind of system of evaluation and feedback. Band grades are too often based solely on attendance and class participation. Although these are important aspects of the evaluation process, students' grades should also reflect the learning that has taken place. Written and ear-training tests as well as playing exams should be an integral part of the total evaluation. Playing exams can be taped in a practice room, so that a student may leave the rehearsal and play the exam in private. To diminish students' anxiety about playing individually for a grade, you might want to allow exams to be repeated until the student is satisfied with his or her performance and grade. Establish a time after which further retakes are not permitted.

Keep in mind when giving grades that you are evaluating each student's progress, not always the finished product. Helping students set individual goals for improvement and giving frequent feedback are excellent ways to motivate both the inexperienced and the most talented students. Try not to compare students, but rather, measure each individual's progress. If you find that a particular student is having difficulty, arrange time to work with him or her individually.

Program Accountability

As we move toward the twenty-first century, more emphasis is being placed on competency testing and program accountability in education. Funding often depends on the success of a program, with success defined in terms of test results. As a music educator, it is critical to clearly articulate objectives and to measure and report the learning that has taken place in the classroom and throughout the program. Music teachers too often take the position that many of the objectives of the music program are not measurable. It is true that some objectives are more easily stated and measured than others, but with some effort nearly all objectives can be identified and evaluated.

The skills involved in some tasks are very easily stated and measured. For example, a reasonable objective for the end of a semester might be, "Students will be able to play from memory all twelve major scales at the tempo of a quarter note = 120." This objective could be measured by a playing exam. Grades could be based on the number of errors and the adherence to tempo requirements.

Other objectives that are very important in music education may be more difficult to measure. One criticism of competency testing in music is that the most valuable components of music education cannot be objectively measured. Although this is true to a certain extent, subjective elements can be identified and evaluated. For example, an objective for the jazz band for the semester might be, "Students will become familiar with and gain an appreciation for a variety of jazz artists and styles." To measure this objective, you might ask each student on the first day of class to identify the ten musical selections he or she would want as the only music available for the rest of his or her life. Ask the same question at the end of the semester to determine if any changes have occurred in students' selections that can be attributed to the listening and performing that has taken place in class. Although this is not objective measurement, it can be inferred that the objective has been met to one degree or another if some jazz selections are chosen by students at the end of the semester that were not chosen on the first day. In addition to giving you some insight as to each student's progress, this comparison could help you evaluate the success of your course and, if necessary, adjust your approach for the next year.

Be prepared to justify the existence of your jazz band or even your entire music program to parents, administration, and community members. You will be able to present a strong argument in behalf of your program if you can clearly state objectives and give concrete evidence of frequent and careful evaluation. In times of educational reform, every music educator must be a strong advocate for the profession. Individual program accountability is an excellent place to start.

Chapter 2

A Quick Lesson in Jazz Styles

Many instrumental music teachers faced with teaching jazz band have had limited experience in performing jazz music. In addition, undergraduate music education course work often puts little emphasis on jazz pedagogy. It is understandable that this lack of background and preparation causes some anxiety for the teacher. It is important to remember that jazz is music. It consists of the same elements that make up other styles of music. Fundamentals of tone production, intonation, rhythmic and pitch accuracy, articulation, balance, sonority, and musicianship apply to teaching jazz band just as they do in concert band and orchestra.

All of the skills that you have learned about teaching music can and should be used in teaching jazz band. It is important to identify year-long goals for the jazz band and to break these goals down into workable weekly and daily objectives. Plan your rehearsals efficiently with time spent each week on jazz listening, aural skill development, jazz theory, improvisation, and sight-reading. Prepare for rehearsal by studying scores and identifying potential problems.

One of the best ways for you as a teacher to become familiar with jazz styles is to begin collecting big band recordings and listening to them. There are many fine professional big band recordings to use as models for your own band. Most of the older big band albums are being re-released on compact disc. Six excellent recordings to get you started are the following:

- Count Basie—*April In Paris*
- The Count Basie Orchestra—*Live at Morocco 1992*
- Stan Kenton—*Kenton '76*
- Woody Herman—*The 40th Anniversary Carnegie Hall Concert*
- Thad Jones—*Consummation*
- Buddy Rich—*Live on King Street*

Take the time to really listen to these albums, concentrating on articulation, time feel, style of the eighth note, balance and sonority of the horns, and the role of the rhythm section. Compare different styles of tunes on an album, then compare the style of one band to another. Try to determine what musical skills are necessary to achieve the performances that you hear. Analyze what each member of the rhythm section is doing to create the time feel of a tune. Listen with particular attention to horn articulations and eighth-note style.

There are some fundamental differences between jazz band music and concert band music. These differences include time feel, style of the eighth note, articulation, the role of the rhythm section, and the use of improvisation. A brief discussion of each of these areas should get you started. Expanding your jazz listening and referring to the materials listed in Chapter 8 will help you continue to develop your skills as a jazz band director.

Time Feel and Eighth-Note Interpretation

Time feel and proper interpretation of the eighth note are critical in establishing the style of a jazz tune. One critical issue is whether the eighth notes are played "straight" or "swung." In any swing-style tune, regardless of tempo, the eighth notes should be "swung," although as the tempo increases the eighth note is played more evenly. The term "swing eighth notes" refers to playing eighth notes unevenly—often following an understood triplet pulse. All other styles, including rock, funk, and all Latin styles, should be played with "straight"—or as written—eighth notes.

The style and metronome marking are usually indicated at the top of the conductor's score in published jazz band music. For example:

- Swing = 144
  or
- Rock = 120

If there is no indication on the conductor's score, the style and tempo might be written at the top of the drum part. If you find no guidance as to tempo and style, you should try to find a recording of the tune or analyze the written rhythmic figures to determine style and tempo. Many times it is difficult to judge if a ballad should be swung or not. Check drum parts to see if the ride cymbal pattern consists primarily of triplets or eighth notes. Triplet patterns indicate swing, as do dotted eighth and sixteenth patterns. Many ballads are played primarily with a straight eighth-note feel. Sometimes only a measure or a short section in a ballad should be swung.

Swing music from the 1930s and 1940s calls for more separation in the swing eighth note. As an example, listen to Benny Goodman's solo on *Sing, Sing, Sing*. More contemporary swing music has a more even, legato feel, though eighth notes are still swung. As an example, listen to the eighth-note style in *Tiptoe* on the Thad Jones–Mel Lewis album *Consummation*. Listen to a variety of styles of swing tunes from different eras and compare the eighth-note feel. Use these as models in your teaching.

Time feel is a very difficult concept to discuss and teach. Playing notes on, ahead, or behind the beat is a factor in time feel. Unlike classical music, jazz seldom uses accelerandos or ritards. Steady time intensifies the harmonic tension and release in jazz. It is the essence of excellent jazz performance. Listen again to the Count Basie *April in Paris* album, concentrating on time feel in the rhythm section, horns, and soloists. Compare this album to the Kenton album, then Buddy Rich, and see if you can hear the concept of playing on, ahead, and behind the beat.

Even the finest professional jazz musicians are constantly striving to improve their mastery of time. Everyone in the band must be conscious of playing with good time, not only the rhythm section. Good time is also a critical part of improvised solos. The abstract concept of time is a fundamental that must be addressed continuously in rehearsals, much as you would address tone production, breath support, and technique—it will improve gradually with consistent work.

Jazz Articulation

When listening to jazz bands perform at concerts, festivals, and competitions, the ones that are most enjoyable involve the audience with the music by creating different moods and by communicating emotion. An essential element in this communication is jazz articulation—the element that gives meaning to the notes on the page. Jazz articulation is one of the cornerstones upon which the language of jazz is built. The musical term "articulation" includes several components. A musician must decide if a note is to be tongued or slurred, how hard or explosive the attack should be, and, perhaps most important, how and when the note should end. Unlike articulation in most concert band music, correct jazz articulation often calls for ending a note with the tongue. Precise articulation makes the ensemble sound tight (cohesive) and contributes to the rhythmic energy, just as in concert band.

In swing-style tunes, the use of scat syllables is an excellent way to achieve precision in articulation. "Scat syllables" refers to nonsense syllables used by jazz singers when improvising. Saying or singing figures using scat syllables helps musical phrases become more precise and take on meaning. Specific suggestions for rehearsing with scat syllables are included in Chapter 4. Listen again to your big band recordings, concentrating on articulation. Compare kinds of attacks and releases and length of notes from tune to tune and from band to band. As you work with your own band, use these professional recordings as models. Learn to make articulation decisions based on what you hear as musically correct. There is not always one right way to interpret a tune. The important thing is that everyone is articulating together in a manner that makes musical sense.

Improvisation

Improvisation is a vital part of jazz. In fact, some would argue that improvisation is the very definition of jazz. It is false advertising to call an ensemble a "jazz band" without incorporating improvisation. "Stage band," "dance band," or "swing band" would be more appropriate labels. Teaching students to improvise is one of the more frightening aspects of teaching jazz band, but the rewards are well worth the effort. Learning to improvise provides students the opportunity for creative development and individual expression.

If you have no background in jazz improvisation, it is important to remember that you *do* know something about music theory and that you *can* guide your students and learn with them. Begin by helping students become comfortable with improvising short phrases and by introducing scales and chords.

At some point you should spend some time becoming more comfortable with teaching improvisation. A good book to get you started is Jerry Coker's *Improvising Jazz.* It is helpful to have some jazz keyboard skills to use in your teaching. *Jazz/Rock Voicings for the Contemporary Keyboard Player* is an excellent source for development of keyboard skills. Also be sure to listen to recordings of the jazz "greats" on all instruments—a listening list is included in Chapter 8—and be sure to take advantage of any clinics or workshops offered at jazz festivals or through schools in your area. Intensive summer workshops such as Jamey Aebersold's summer improvisation camps, the University of Wisconsin's Shell Lake Jazz Camp, or Eastman School of Music's Summer Program are outstanding ways to become more proficient at teaching jazz band and improvisation. Many times these programs can be taken for credit, which can be applied to an advanced degree or used to update your teacher's license.

The Rhythm Section

A fundamentally sound rhythm section is the key element to a good jazz band. The responsibilities of the rhythm section include:

- Maintaining consistent time (not rushing or dragging)
- Establishing the proper style and feel
- Generating excitement
- Defining the form and harmonic structure of the music
- Preparing rhythmic figures in the horns
- Functioning as soloists

Developing a good jazz rhythm section presents the biggest problem for most band directors, as they often have little knowledge of how to play or teach these instruments. Also, the piano, bass, drums, and guitar play very different roles from the horns in the jazz band.

Many times the students in the rhythm section have not been members of an organized band program before entering the jazz band. Piano, bass, and guitar players usually have had some private instruction, but their backgrounds and experiences are very different from the students who began their instruments in a school band program. Rhythm players often have outstanding aural skills but do not read music very well. Even if they do read written parts well, they often do not know how to read jazz chord symbols. These "gaps" in their music education must be addressed if the rhythm section is going to function properly. Following is a short discussion of each of these instruments to help you get started. An excellent resource for additional information is *Guide for the Modern Jazz Rhythm Section* by Steve Houghton.

Piano

When selecting a pianist for jazz band, look for a student who plays classical piano well (assuming you do not have an accomplished jazz pianist). Critical factors are rhythmic accuracy, steady time feel, and a command of major scales. Some background in music theory is very helpful.

When the pianist is playing a written part (musical notation), the biggest concern is style. The piano nearly always functions as a staccato percussion instrument in the jazz band. The pedal *should not* be used except for rare special effects. The pianist must listen to and match horn articulations in most passages. Not all published parts are well written. They are frequently much too "busy" and rhythmically thick, with the piano doubling the bass part in the left hand. As a rule, the bass line should not be doubled, root position chords should be avoided, and the piano should play lightly with short, well placed rhythmic punches. The pianist must learn to "edit" written out parts to achieve the desired effect.

Learning to "comp," or construct chords from chord symbols when no written-out part is provided, should be a long-term goal of the pianist. Begin by having the student write out the notes in each chord in root position. Here are a few simple guidelines for the voicing of chords that will sound "hip" or stylistically appropriate to jazz:

- Never play chords in root position, stacking 3rds (1-3-5-7).
- Use voice dominant 7th chords 3-7-9 or 7-3-13 (the 9 and 13 can always be added for color).
- Minor seventh chords can be easily voiced 3-5-7-9.
- As a rule, keep chords above the E below middle C.

- Try to achieve smooth voice leading by interchanging voicing.
- Do not play the root of the chord in the bass.
- Listen to professional recordings of the styles called for and try to copy what you hear.

Bass

A bass player is essential in the jazz band. Keyboard bass is a poor substitute for electric or acoustic bass and should be avoided if at all possible. The bass provides the rhythmic foundation for the rhythm section and the band. Ideally, the acoustic bass should be used for most jazz styles, as the physical nature of the instrument provides the correct rhythmic feel as well as the desired decay of tone. Investing in good equipment for your bass player should be a financial priority for the jazz program.

When selecting a bass player for jazz band, look for a student who plays bass or guitar in a rock band or a bass player from orchestra (assuming you do not have an accomplished jazz bassist). If none of these exists, then select a good student from your concert band who is interested in learning to play the bass. In any case, the most important attributes the student should have are strong rhythmic ability and a very good sense of time. The ability to read bass clef and some theory background is helpful.

An electric bass is relatively simple to play. If you are starting a beginner on bass, obviously some private instruction would be very helpful. If this is not possible, buy a good beginning bass method and set aside an hour a week to guide the student's progress, helping establish good hand position and good right hand technique. Be sure that the student is exerting physical effort or "digging into" the strings, and not relying mainly on the amplification for tone. In good bass playing, rhythmic energy is an important factor that is often over-looked by the young player.

While the student is learning the fundamentals of bass playing, use a keyboard bass (select two pianists) in your band rehearsals, with the new bass player playing along without amplification. As the bass player progresses, allow him or her to play "out loud" on the tunes he or she can handle. Your goal is to replace the keyboard bass entirely as soon as possible.

An orchestral bass player will generally know the basics of playing the instrument and reading music, but will need to learn correct right-hand technique. Also, much of the music he has encountered in the past will have been in sharp keys, which are more easily approached by young string players.

Rock guitar and bass players will often have excellent technique and good ears, but little training in music reading and ensemble skills. They are often intimidated by how much everyone else seems to know. Work to help them overcome their weaknesses while calling attention to the things they do well. Their aural skills are most likely much more advanced than the other students', and they are usually less inhibited about improvising.

The bass functions in the rhythm section as the center of the rhythmic pulse for the band. It also outlines the harmonic structure of the music. It is important to remember that the bass is a legato instrument in swing style music. Each quarter note should lead to the next both melodically and rhythmically. The most common mistake young bass players make is playing with too many leaps and too much separation.

Much of the music published for school jazz bands will have written out bass parts, however you may encounter some bass parts that are only chord symbols. Certainly, as your bass player develops, she or he should learn to construct bass lines from chord symbols. An excellent text that deals with bass line construction is *The Bottom Line* by Todd Coolman. A few simple guidelines may help:

- Almost all swing bass lines "walk" in continuous legato quarter notes.
- The root of the chord is usually played on the downbeat or on beats one and three if there are two changes in a measure.
- It is good practice to anticipate the next chord by a half or whole step above or below the root.
- Rock bass lines generally have less harmonic activity and more rhythmic variety—the use of "space" (silence) often makes a rock bass line more "hip."
- Most Latin bass lines concentrate on the root and fifth of the chord with a repetitive rhythmic figure (i.e., a dotted quarter note followed by an eighth note).
- When playing sections that are in rhythmic unison with the horns, the articulations must match those of the horns.
- Listen to professional recordings of the styles called for and try to copy what you hear.
- Listen to the drummer's high-hat and "lock in" to it.

Drums

When selecting a drummer for the jazz band, the most important criterion is a good sense of time. You will often hear "flashy" drummers who demonstrate considerable technique, but if their time is not steady, they can destroy the band. Although there are usually several drummers in your concert band who have drum-set experience, most will not have much background in playing jazz. A good rock drummer with steady time and a good attitude about learning jazz should easily learn to play swing.

The drummer has several responsibilities in the jazz band. First and foremost, he must establish and maintain a steady tempo with the correct style. Second, he must delineate the form of the tune. He must know the overall form (ABA, AABA, and so on), as well as the number of measures in each phrase, and be able to communicate this knowledge to the band and the audience through his playing. This can be done by marking phrases and sections with fills, changing cymbals or dynamics, and by altering rhythmic patterns. Third, he should anticipate and set up rhythmic figures that occur in the horns to add rhythmic excitement and help achieve rhythmic precision throughout the band. Steve Houghton's *Studio and Big Band Drumming* is an excellent guide. Following are some tips for the jazz drummer:

- Listen to and play with the lead trumpet player and bass player at all times.
- The high-hat and ride cymbals are the most important components of the drum set when playing jazz.
- On a 4/4 swing tune, the high hat should *always* be played aggressively on 2 and 4.
- The slower the tempo of a tune, the more subdivision is required.
- The eighth-note style should be clearly and aggressively played on the ride cymbal, and the pattern should "lock" precisely with the bass line.
- Play lightly on the bass drum emulating the bass.
- Keep fills and setups simple and *in time*—most students try to play too much.
- Use the written drum part as a guideline only—listen to and study the tune to edit and enhance.
- Refer to the lead trumpet part, which is often a better guide than the drum part, for rhythms and articulations.
- Memorize the form of the tune as soon as possible so that you can mark off phrases and choruses.
- Listen to professional recordings of various styles.
- Know the appropriate style—don't fake it.
- Practice with a tape recorder and headphones, playing along with professional recordings to improve time and style.
- Record your own playing and listen for temporal tendencies such as rushing and dragging.

Guitar

If you have a pianist, the guitar is an optional member of the rhythm section. The piano and guitar play essentially the same role in the rhythm section, providing rhythmic energy and outlining the harmonic structure of the tune. A good guitar player can add variety and creativity to the rhythm section. In addition, many guitar players are very good at improvisation and can add a great deal to the band as soloists, particularly on rock or funk tunes.

If you have both piano and guitar, you must make certain that they do not get in each other's way. If both the piano and guitar are comping on a tune, it often sounds cluttered and muddy, both rhythmically and harmonically. The easiest way to avoid this problem is to have them trade choruses or even tunes. If time is spent working out voicings and rhythmic patterns, it is possible to use both together.

Most young guitar players are essentially rock musicians who have learned to play either through private instruction or by listening. Many will have outstanding aural skills. Often they are able to read basic changes in sharp keys, but do not know the more complex chords called for in jazz band music. Jazz band guitar parts are primarily sequences of chord changes that require the guitarist to comp.

A jazz guitar chord book such as Mickey Baker's *Complete Course in Jazz Guitar* will be necessary to help your guitarist learn chords and voicings for jazz band. You will also want to help him or her develop a concept of tone quality appropriate for jazz band. Sometimes the guitar part will have a written out melodic line. If your guitarist does not read notation, this should be a goal for individual development. Following are some suggestions for getting started:

- Develop concept of tone quality appropriate to jazz playing.
- Learn to read written pitches and rhythms.
- Chords should be played on all four beats of the measure using a downstroke in older swing tunes.
- Chords should be placed on two and four in contemporary swing tunes of a moderate tempo.
- Chords should be placed on one and three in very fast swing tunes.
- Melodic lines that are in unison with the horns should be articulated in the same manner as the horns.

Working Together

The rhythm section must work together as a unit. Musical communication must be established among the members of the rhythm section by listening to each other at all times and reacting musically to what is heard. Good balance, cohesive time feel, creative enhancement of the music, and interplay with the band and soloists are all necessary components of a good rhythm section. The very best way to understand the complex responsibilities of the rhythm section in jazz is by listening to professional recordings of big bands and combos.

Chapter 3

Materials and Equipment

The field of jazz education has experienced incredible growth in the past twenty years. There was a time when good published jazz band music was rare, as were materials for teaching improvisation. Today, you will find a wealth of instructional materials, recordings, videos, and good playable jazz band music. As most of us work within a limited budget, it is important to have long-term goals in mind to build the jazz music library, instructional library, and listening library and to spend money as efficiently as possible.

Selecting Music for Concerts and Festivals

One of the most important factors to successful jazz band performance is the selection of music. Planning a program that meets the educational needs of the students should be the number one priority; however, audience appeal must also be considered. The publication of good literature for the jazz band has mushroomed in the past twenty years, with excellent music available for bands at all levels. A number of factors should be taken into consideration when programming for the jazz band:

■ Variety of tempo and style—Medium to up-tempo swing tunes should make up the bulk of your jazz band literature; however, every program should include some contrasting tunes. A rock or swing ballad and at least one rock, funk, or Latin tune should be included. A swing or rock shuffle can also add variety.

■ Variety of key and form—Your audience will tire of hearing tunes that are all alike (such as B♭ blues), and your students will not be challenged to expand their technical ability, improvisation, and understanding of musical form. A tune in AABA song form (many jazz arrangements of show tunes or bebop standards are AABA) or a rock tune in ABA form will interest your audience and will work as an educational tool.

■ Variety of composers and arrangers—Except for special occasions when you might want to feature music of a classic jazz composer, it is best not to program too many charts by the same composer or arranger. (Even an all-Nestico program would get old!)

■ Difficulty—Select some tunes that are relatively easy for your band to prepare. These will build confidence and allow time for detailed work on musicianship and style. One or two more difficult works should be included to stretch the band's technical growth.

■ Improvisation opportunities—At least one tune might feature an outstanding soloist who is either a member of the ensemble or a guest. One or two charts should be selected to be "opened up," allowing several students the opportunity to improvise. Rock charts with simple changes and blues tunes work very well for this purpose.

■ Strengths and weaknesses—If you have a particularly strong section or individual, you may want to choose a tune that features this strength. In some cases you may want to hide weaknesses (festivals, community performances, and so on), but sometimes choosing a chart that addresses a particular weakness can really pay off educationally.

■ Recorded examples—Choose some tunes for which quality recordings are available. Listening to a good professional recording of a tune will help the band internalize style, and will give the soloists ideas to draw from for their own improvisation.

■ Quality of music—The jazz band (big band) is a musical ensemble with a rich history dating from the 1920s. A great deal of very high quality literature is available. Keep this in mind as you select music, always asking yourself if the chart you've chosen has musical integrity, and if it is music that you like and want to listen to.

■ Vocals—There are many good published vocal charts. Consider featuring a solo vocalist from time to time.

■ Program order—Once you have selected music, a program order must be established that presents a satisfying total package. Following are sample programs for both middle and high school bands.

Middle School Program

Cozy Toes ....Lennie Neihaus
    Easy medium swing tune. This is a good opening selection.

Mr. Basket ....Matt Harris
    Funk tune that works well for young band. Change of style. Could use multiple soloists.

Here's That Rainy Day ....arr. Curnow
    Easier arrangement of this famous ballad that captures the lushness of the Kenton band.

Grenada Smoothie ....arr. Mark Taylor
    Young band arrangement of a great samba.

Jumpin' at the Woodside ....arr. Sammy Nestico
    Young band arrangement of this Count Basie classic. Great closer.

High School Program

Basie Straight...Sammy Nestico
   Medium swing opener that is not too difficult but provides a solid
   opening. Sax soli. Professional recording available

St. Thomas.................................Sonny Rollins, arr. Matt Taylor
   A good arrangement of a standard samba. Provides a strong con-
   trast to the opener. This tune can be opened up for multiple
   soloists

Concerto for Cootie...Duke Ellington
   A jazz classic featuring trumpet solo. Style will be a challenge for
   the band. It offers a change of mood and presents a historical
   piece. A professional recording is available.

Bubblehead..Denis DiBlasio
   This is a medium tempo blues that is moderately easy, but exciting.
   It can also be used to feature several soloists.

Looking Back...Tom Kubis
   A moderately difficult rock ballad that features tenor saxophone. It
   changes the mood, tempo, and style and effectively sets up the
   closing tune.

Us ....Thad Jones
   Medium difficult funk/rock tune that showcases the trombone section. It builds in intensity to close the program. A professional
   recording is available.

Some suggested composers and arrangers for both young bands
and intermediate high school groups are listed below. Most of these
writers also have more difficult material that works well for an
advanced high school band.

- Al Cobine
- Matt Harris
- Roger Holmes
- Frank Mantooth

- Sammy Nestico
- Roger Pemberton
- Dominic Spera
- Mark Taylor

Other composers and arrangers for the more advanced band:

- Matt Catingub
- Bob Florence
- Bill Holman
- Thad Jones

- Tom Kubis
- John LaBarbera
- Neil Slater

Since you probably do not have an unlimited amount of money to
spend, it is important to select jazz band music carefully. Though it
may be tempting (and at times appropriate) to perform an arrange-

ment of a pop tune, think carefully about the long-term value of purchasing material of this type. Try to find an opportunity to hear a tune before making a purchase. Many publishers will send demonstration tapes on request, and new music is performed at state and national conventions, jazz festivals, and university jazz band concerts. If you are not able to listen to a tune before making a purchase, look for an unbiased review of the tune in a professional magazine, or go to your local music store and study the score. Look for opportunities to borrow music from colleagues when possible, especially for sight-reading purposes. When you find a chart you really like, purchase it for your library. See Chapter 8 for a list of catalogs of jazz music. Many vendors have knowledgeable salespeople who will answer questions over the telephone. Do not hesitate to call for information about ranges, difficulty level, or even suggestions about material that might be appropriate for your band.

Improvisation Materials

Many teachers find it very helpful to use a class method for teaching improvisation. Three methods especially appropriate for the young player are *DiBlasio's Bop Shop* by Denis DiBlasio and *Blues and the Basics* and *Stretching Out* by Dominic Spera. Both of these authors approach improvisation in a very practical and straightforward manner that allows students to achieve results rapidly.

You will want to begin to build a library of supplementary materials as well. Jamey Aebersold publishes more than fifty volumes of play-along book-and-recording sets that include tunes of most of the jazz greats. The books have the melody and chord changes of tunes for B♭, E♭, C treble clef, and C bass clef instruments. The recordings are of professional rhythm sections playing the accompaniment with which students can practice playing the tunes and improvising. Stereo separation, with the bass and drums in the left channel and the piano or guitar in the right channel, makes these play-alongs useful for rhythm players as well. Two volumes that are especially good for beginners are Volume 1—*Jazz: How to Play and Improvise* and Volume 24—*Major and Minor*. In addition to these, a basic play-along library might include:

- Volume 21—*Getting It Together*
- Volume 2—*Nothin' But the Blues*
- Volume 3—*The II/V7/I Progression*
- Volume 54—*Maiden Voyage*
- Volume 32—*Ballads*

These may be ordered directly from Jamey Aebersold (see Chapter 8) or purchased through your local music store.

There are many excellent jazz books for individual instruments, ear training, jazz theory, and advanced improvisation. If you are operating on a limited budget, check with your school librarian to see if library funds are available for the purchase of resource materials. If these materials are housed in the school library, it will be convenient for students to check out materials. A good basic improvisation instructional library to supplement the class instruction methods might include:

- *The Jazz Language*—Dan Hearle
- *Improvising Jazz*—Dan Hearle
- *Jazz Improvisation*—David Baker
- *A New Approach to Ear Training*—David Baker
- *Guitar Improvisation*—Barry Galbraith
- *Famous Jazz Guitar Solos*
- *Charlie Parker Omnibook*
- *The Improviser's Bass Method*—Chuck Sher
- *Clifford Brown Complete Transcriptions*
- *J. J. Johnson Solos*
- *Patterns for Jazz*—Jerry Coker
- *Jazz Improvisation*—John Mehegan

Many of these materials will be available through your local music dealer.

Building a Listening Library

Building a listening library should be a long-term goal for your jazz program. Plan to set aside a small portion of your budget each year to buy jazz recordings. Even two or three recordings a year will make a difference. You may also want to look into school library funding for recorded materials. Jazz artists and bands whose recordings should be included in a good basic library are listed in Chapter 8. Sources for ordering jazz recordings are included as well.

There are many excellent jazz videotapes available commercially. These range from instructional tapes such as Louis Bellson's *Beginner's Drum Course* to the *Vintage Jazz Collection,* which includes performances of jazz greats Count Basie, John Coltrane, Duke Ellington, and others. Videos, particularly those that introduce students to great jazz artists of the past, are excellent supplementary material. Submit requests for purchase of videos to your school or public library.

Equipment

You may already own much of the equipment needed to outfit the jazz band. Following is a list of essential items that the school should provide:

- Drum set
- Electric bass or acoustic bass
- Bass amplifier
- Tenor and baritone saxophones

Drum Set

There are several factors to consider when purchasing a drum set for the jazz band. You do not need a large set with multiple toms and cymbals. A basic jazz kit consisting of a small bass drum (20 or 22 inch), a snare drum, a floor tom, and a side tom is appropriate for jazz playing. Cymbals to get you started should include high-hat cymbals, a ride cymbal, and a crash cymbal. You may want to purchase an additional crash cymbal for color and variety. Choose your cymbals carefully, particularly the ride—look for one that has a dark, dry sound for big band playing. In addition to the drums and cymbals, you will need the appropriate hardware, a comfortable seat, and cases. Do not try to save money by eliminating the purchase of cases. Drums should be packed for protection whenever you travel. In the long run, drum cases will save you money. All of the major percussion manufacturers market a jazz drum set. Shop around for the best price.

Bass

The bass is the foundation of the jazz band both rhythmically and harmonically. Investing in good equipment for your bass player is very important. You must first decide if you are going to initially purchase an electric bass or an acoustic bass. If your school has an orchestra program, an acoustic bass may be the best choice. You may find that your school orchestra owns an extra acoustic bass that can be adapted for jazz band.

To adapt a string bass for jazz playing, you must have the bridge cut down so that the strings sit lower, and outfit the bass with flat wound jazz strings rather than the round wound strings that are appropriate for use with a bow. Suggested strings for jazz bass are Tomastick steel core or rope core strings, which are softer and allow the jazz player to achieve a good sound. The bass should have an adjustable bridge, and a pick-up and preamplifier must be purchased so that the bass can be channeled through an amplifier. The Fishman pick-up and preamp do an excellent job. Underwood also makes a good pick-up to amplify the acoustic bass for jazz. If you purchase a string bass, any good 3/4-size student model bass can be adjusted to work well.

If you have no string program in your school, you may want to purchase an electric bass to get started. Although it is not the authentic instrument that should be used in most jazz band music, it is less expensive and easier to learn to play. It is also a much better choice than keyboard bass. The Fender Jazz Bass or Fender Precision Bass are excellent choices.

Bass Amplifier

You will also need a good bass amplifier. Harkey and Galyan Kruger are two excellent brands. The Galyan Kruger "Combo" with a 15-inch speaker is a portable but powerful amplifier that is highly recommended. Do not buy large cabinet speakers. A 100-watt bass amplifier with a 15-inch speaker is sufficient and will achieve the sound desired for the jazz band. Achieving good tone quality from your acoustic or electric bass is extremely important to the overall sound of the jazz band.

Tenor and Baritone Saxophones

Your school may already own tenor and baritone saxophones that can be used in the jazz band. Be sure that these instruments are in good playing condition. Woodwind instruments need regular maintenance and adjustment in order to work properly. If you need to purchase a tenor saxophone, the Leblanc "Vito" is a good student instrument. Yamaha and Couf also make excellent medium-priced instruments—the Yamaha baritone saxophone, for example. You should consider spending the extra money for a low A key on the baritone saxophone, as jazz band music often uses the low register.

Wish List

A great deal of money can be spent on equipment for the jazz band. The items mentioned are essential for getting started. The following items should be considered in a long-term purchase plan that addresses the total program (This wish list is organized from most to least important):

- Jazz saxophone mouthpieces
- Double-trigger bass trombone
- Soprano saxophone
- Acoustic bass or electric bass (whichever was not purchased as basic equipment)
- Auxiliary percussion equipment

- Electronic keyboard or synthesizer and amplifier
- Mutes for brass
- Flügelhorns

Jazz Saxophone Mouthpieces

The mouthpiece and reed setup can make a big difference in your saxophonists' sounds. Saxophonists have a difficult time competing with the volume produced by the brass players in the jazz band. A good jazz mouthpiece will help your saxophonists achieve a characteristic jazz sound that can be heard in the ensemble. It is not a problem for a saxophonist to play on a different mouthpiece in jazz band than he does in concert band. In fact, he will find it much easier to achieve a proper sound in each ensemble if he is playing on an appropriate mouthpiece. It is a good idea for the school to own a set of jazz saxophone mouthpieces.

A hard-rubber Meyer 6 is a good jazz mouthpiece for alto saxophone players. It opens up the sound, but is not too difficult to control. The hard-rubber Meyer 6 is also a good choice for tenor saxophones as is the Berg Larson hard-rubber 125/0. The metal Otto Link 7* or the Yanagasawa 7 are excellent jazz mouthpieces for the baritone saxophone. Be certain that the ligature with the mouthpiece fits well and is in good condition. Rovner ligatures are a good choice for all saxophones.

The reed is also an important factor in achieving good saxophone tone quality. Be certain that good reeds are available for purchase by your saxophonists. If there is not a convenient local music store where reeds can be purchased, perhaps your school bookstore will stock reeds. A medium strength reed, number 2 or 2 1/2, works best with most of the alto and tenor mouthpieces mentioned above. With the baritone saxophone mouthpieces, number 3 reeds are recommended. Rovner makes plastic tenor and baritone saxophone reeds that many professionals use. You may want to have your students try the Rovner plastic reeds, as they are consistent and durable, cutting down on the expense and hassle encountered with cane reeds.

Double Trigger Bass Trombone

Much of the more advanced jazz band music has bass trombone parts that are written in the octave below B♭ below middle C. Some parts cannot be played on a common B♭ trombone with an F attachment. Yamaha, Getzen, and Holton all make a good moderately priced double trigger bass trombone. Be sure that a good bass trombone mouthpiece is included. If your bass trombone player is used to playing tenor trombone, a Bach 5G is a good mouthpiece to use when switching to the bass trombone. If you have a tuba player doubling on bass trombone, the Bach 1G is a very large mouthpiece that will facilitate doubling and achieve an excellent characteristic bass trombone sound.

Soprano Saxophone

Some jazz band music is written for soprano saxophone in place of the lead alto. The soprano saxophone also works well as a solo instrument in the jazz band as it adds a different timbre and color to the band. Among the best brands are the Yamaha or Yanagasawa.

Auxiliary Percussion Equipment

Some of the music that you play in jazz band will use auxiliary percussion instruments. Your school may already own many auxiliary percussion instruments. If not, shop around for the best prices, as most percussion manufacturers will make these products:

- Conga drums
- Bongo drums
- Vibraphone and mallets
- Large and small cowbells
- Claves
- Maracas
- Vibraslap
- Wind chimes or bell tree
- Cabasa

It is a good idea to place smaller percussion instruments in a trap case with an inventory list included so that these instruments do not get misplaced.

Electronic Keyboard or Synthesizer

The Korg M-1 or 01W are very popular keyboards that can be used in the jazz band and can also interface with a computer. Roland and Ensoniq also make excellent keyboards and synthesizers. Technology changes very rapidly, so it is advisable to do some research before purchasing a synthesizer. Identify the applications for which the synthesizer will be used and shop carefully for the best piece of equipment for your situation. Endless educational opportunities exist when the synthesizer is interfaced with a computer. Software that is both fun and exciting for students to use is available for note reading, ear training, composition, and improvisation.

Keyboard Amplifier

Any standard keyboard amplifier will be adequate for use with the jazz band. Consider buying an amplifier that is relatively portable and versatile, such as the standard Peavy keyboard amplifier.

Trumpet and Trombone Mutes

You may want to ask your trumpet and trombone players to purchase some or all of the mutes required for jazz band. Mutes are used to achieve a different tone color or a special effect. It is important that all players use the proper mute indicated in the music. Mixing brands of mutes within the section can ruin the effect of a muted passage, as using various brands of mutes can sound very different. If you have some extra money to spend, it would be nice to have sets of the same brand mutes to be used by the brass players in jazz band. Remind students to adjust the tuning slide when playing with a mute. A straight or harmon mute usually causes the instrument to play sharp, while cup and bucket mutes cause the instrument to play flat. Following are some suggested brands of mutes:

- Trumpet straight mute—Vacchiano or Tom Crown (copper bottom). Do not buy a fiber or cardboard straight mute.
- Trumpet cup mute—Stonelined.
- Trumpet harmon mute—Jo-Ral (called a "bubble mute"). Be sure that the stem is removed from the harmon mute. The only time the harmon mute is played with the stem in is to achieve a "toy trumpet" effect or in old style Dixieland music.
- Trumpet plunger—Purchase a 4-inch diameter plunger from the hardware store and remove the handle.
- Trombone straight mute—Jo-Ral or Tom Crown (metal). Do not buy a fiber or cardboard straight mute.
- Trombone cup and bucket mutes—Stonelined.
- Trombone plunger—purchase a six-inch diameter plunger from the hardware store and remove the handle.

Flügelhorns

Occasionally, jazz band music calls for the use of flügelhorns by one or all of the trumpet players. Although it is acceptable to play the part on trumpets, flügelhorns add a new color to the jazz band. The flügelhorn is often used as a solo instrument as well. Yamaha makes a good flügelhorn that is moderately priced.

Chapter 4

Rehearsal Techniques

Physical Setup

The "stacked" setup is the most common configuration for the horns in a jazz band. Figures 1 and 2 illustrate two effective seating arrangements. Notice that in both cases the lead players from each section form a line down the middle of the band. The setup in figure 1 works well if you have strong baritone saxophone and bass trombone players. Placing these instruments on the opposite side from the rhythm section frames the band with the

FIGURE 1					
		Trumpet II	Trumpet I	Trumpet III	Trumpet IV	4 trumpet parts
(Trumpet) III			(Trumpet) IV	(Trumpet) V	5 trumpet parts
	Trombone II	Trombone I	Trombone III	Trombone IV	4 trombone parts
(Trombone) III			(Trombone) IV	(Trombone V or Tuba)	5 trombone parts
Tenor Saxophone I	Alto Saxophone II	Alto Saxophone I	Tenor Saxophone II	Baritone Saxophone	

(Left side, top to bottom: BASS, DRUM, PIANO, GUITAR)

FIGURE 2					
Trumpet IV	Trumpet III	Trumpet I	Trumpet II		4 trumpet parts
(Trumpet) V	(Trumpet) IV			(Trumpet) III	5 trumpet parts
Trombone IV	Trombone III	Trombone I	Trombone II		4 trombone parts
(Trombone V or Tuba)	(Trombone) IV			(Trombone) III	5 trombone parts
Baritone Saxophone	Tenor Saxophone II	Alto Saxophone I	Alto Saxophone II	Tenor Saxophone I	

(Left side, top to bottom: BASS, DRUMS, PIANO, GUITAR)

bass on one side and the low winds on the other. If your baritone saxophone and bass trombone are inexperienced players, you may want to place them near the bass to improve intonation and rhythmic precision (figure 2).

If you rehearse in a room with risers, seat the saxophones on the first level and have the trombones and trumpets stand on the next two levels. If there are no risers in your room, seat the saxophones and the trombones and have the trumpets stand.

It is critical to place the rhythm section as close to the horns as possible. The piano, bass, drums, and guitar should also be close to each other and should be able to see one another. Physical proximity and eye contact are important factors in achieving precision in the rhythm section.

An excellent way to improve style and precision throughout the entire ensemble is to rehearse in a box (figure 3). In this configuration, all of the players can hear and see one another. You should notice improvement in note length, articulation, style, balance, and phrasing very quickly when rehearsing in this setup.

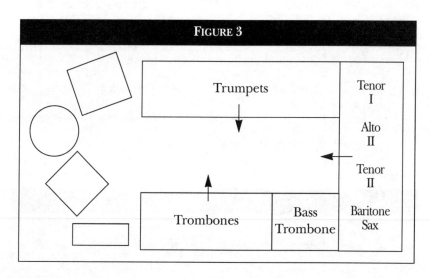

FIGURE 3

Establishing the Proper Learning Atmosphere

One of your most important responsibilities as a teacher is to create an atmosphere in which effective learning can take place. There are many factors that contribute to the classroom learning atmosphere. Even though jazz band may be an extracurricular ensemble and is certainly a more relaxed situation than a large marching or concert band, you must manage student behavior and maintain a climate of mutual respect. Here are some suggestions for creating the proper rehearsal atmosphere:

Getting Started with Jazz Band

- Post and enforce a few simple classroom rules, such as:
    1. Be in your seats with instruments out and ready to play on time.
    2. No individual warm-up. Wait to warm up with the band.
    3. No gum.
    4. Show respect for your teacher and peers by listening without talking or playing when others are speaking.
    5. Maintain proper posture when playing your instrument.
- Always start rehearsal on time.
- Work announcements and business items into the rehearsal and keep them as brief as possible.
- Remind a student only once in class when a discipline problem occurs; then speak to the student individually after class.
- Don't be afraid to send a student to the principal's office if his or her behavior is interfering with other students' learning.
- Avoid serious problems by dealing fairly and consistently with everyday annoyances.
- If repeated rule infractions occur or serious problems develop, call the student's parents to discuss the difficulty.
- Talk with the school guidance counselor, other teachers, or the principal for suggestions and help in dealing with problems.
- Make your room a pleasant environment for learning by keeping it clean and neat.
- Use bulletin board space for interesting and attractive displays. Dedicate some bulletin board space to the jazz band with articles and record reviews, photos of your band, and pictures and biographies of jazz artists. Encourage students to bring in interesting jazz materials for display. Change bulletin board materials frequently.
- Respect your students—be positive and encouraging.
- Ask students for suggestions and listen carefully to their ideas and concerns. Implement students' suggestions whenever it is practical.
- Conduct an organized and motivating rehearsal every day. If you do your best, students will respond.

Jazz Band Warm-Ups

The purpose of any good warm-up is to physically and mentally prepare for rehearsal or performance. A warm-up should address the fundamentals of playing—tone quality, breath support, intonation, and technique. You can also use the warm-up time to teach scales and jazz patterns and to work on ear training.

You might begin the warm-up with a scale played in whole notes. Play the scale ascending to the ninth and back down again. Have the drummer accompany the band with swing time (see music example 1).

Music Example 1

ride cymbal
high-hat
bass drum

Remind students to use proper breath support and to strive for the best possible tone quality. Also ask students to listen to intonation and adjust pitch to the best of their ability. Introduce one or two new scales each week, working through all of the major scales, then move on to dorian, mixolydian, pentatonic, and blues scales. You can teach the scales by rote or have students read them from scales sheets or from a class improvisation book such as *Stretching Out* by Dominic Spera. Students should be asked to memorize scales.

The circle of 4ths (see figure 4) is a good tool for teaching key signatures. It also provides a good foundation for the understanding of harmonic function. Students should memorize the circle of fourths and practice scales in this order.

FIGURE 4

Circle of
fourths

F   Bb ↘   Eb

C   Ab

G   Db

D   Gb

A   Cb

E   (B)

Continue the warm-up with scales (see music example 2) or jazz patterns (see music example 3) played in eighth notes to develop technique and swing eighth-note style. Once again the drummer should accompany the warm-up with swing time. As students develop facility, play the scales or patterns in all of the keys around the circle of fourths.

Getting Started with Jazz Band

Music Example 2

continue
through
the circle
of fourths

Music Example 3

Conclude the warm-up by playing a portion of a ballad that involves the entire band playing in rhythmic unison. Focus the students' attention on balance, intonation, phrasing, rhythmic precision, and style. Some suggested tunes:

- *Lil' Darlin*—Neil Hefti
- *Bess You Is My Woman*—arr. by Roger Pemberton
- *Jamie*—Sammy Nestico
- *Dreamsville*—Henry Mancini/arr. by John Higgins (good for middle school)

Tuning the Band

Good intonation is very important in jazz band just as it is in any musical group. Too often young players (and even some directors) think that intonation is not important when playing jazz. Although the use of an electronic tuner will not solve all intonation problems, it is a good tool to help students tune to a common pitch and to become familiar with the intonation tendencies of their individual instruments. It is a good idea to check the intonation on more than one note. With the use of an electronic tuner, check the following notes in each section:

- Saxophones—A and B♭ concert in the lower and upper octaves
- Trombones—fourth line F, B♭ above the staff, and 2nd line B♭ .
- Trumpets—F, G, A, B♭ concert—Have the trumpet players slur these notes. If you have a strong lead player who is frequently playing in the upper register, check these same pitches in the upper register.

Be sure that your tuner is calibrated to the pitch of the piano. The bass and guitar can plug directly into the tuner and tune each string.

Occasionally, take time to work on intonation in depth. Following are some activities that may help students develop better intonation:

Intonation Activity Number One. With students working in pairs, have one student slowly play each note of the chromatic scale over the entire range of his instrument. Using an electronic tuner, the other student should chart each pitch, indicating if it is flat, in tune, or sharp. Provide the students with a worksheet of the chromatic scale with columns to record intonation from - 2 (very flat) to 0 (in tune) to + 2 (very sharp). The student who is playing should not look at the tuner or try to adjust intonation by ear. Initially this exercise is intended to provide the student with information about the inherent intonation tendencies of his particular instrument. After every student has completed the activity once, it can be repeated with an effort made to adjust intonation. This activity could be done in class or as a homework assignment and should be repeated occasionally to reinforce the responsibility of individuals to play in tune.

Intonation Activity Number Two. In full band rehearsal or sectionals, ask individual students to try to match a pitch generated by an electronic tuner. You can also ask another member of the band to play a pitch, but keep in mind that the pitch to be matched must remain constant. First the student should listen to the pitch to be matched, then play along. Ask the student to make the adjustment he feels is called for and then play along with the pitch again. Have him repeat the process until he feels he is in tune.

Intonation Activity Number Three. Select a chord from one of the tunes that you are rehearsing that is harmonized throughout the entire horn section. Write the notes of the chord on the chalk board and ask each student to determine which chord tone he is assigned (1, 3, 5, 7, and so on). Have the students who are playing the third of the chord attempt to play as flat as possible. Then ask them to adjust to playing the third as sharp as possible, and finally adjust to playing in tune. Manipulate each chord tone in this manner to demonstrate to the students the sound of the chord when it is in tune.

Balance within and between Sections

Along with tone quality and intonation, balance is a critical ensemble skill that contributes to the overall sonority or sound of the band. With only one player per part, it is especially important that every member of the band contribute with a good full sound. The two most common balance problems are not enough sound from the inner parts and the muddy effect created when students have no concept of the relative importance of each part.

Ask the band to think of the lead trumpet and bass trombone/baritone saxophone as the framework within which the rest of the horns must work. All of the other horns should always listen and play within this framework, coming up to but never exceeding the volume of these players. To help students hear and understand proper ensemble balance, have one or two students play very loudly while the rest of the band plays very softly. Experiment with different combinations to demonstrate to the students that improper balance can be heard and corrected.

Blaring or out-of-control playing occurs when students attempt to play at levels louder than they can physically control. While individuals should constantly work to develop larger, fuller sounds, fine ensemble playing depends on critical listening for balance and control.

The bass trombone and baritone saxophone often play the same part. They usually provide the harmonic foundation for the horn section and should generally play a little stronger than the other horns. Good intonation and blend between the bass trombone and baritone saxophone will contribute to a solid foundation and proper balance.

Guidelines for proper balance that are useful in any musical ensemble also apply to the jazz band. For example:

- Bring out the moving lines.
- Play longer accompaniment notes softer so that melodic lines can be heard.
- Play unison passages softer than harmonized passages unless marked otherwise.
- Balance among the members of the rhythm section and between the rhythm section and the horns is another factor that must be considered in the jazz band.
- Take time to experiment with the volume on the amplifier for the bass, guitar, and keyboard. Write down the settings that achieve the desired results, and be sure that students maintain these levels in rehearsal.
- In general, the drummer should play his cymbals aggressively, but should take care not to play too loudly on the bass drum, snare, or toms.
- Many times dynamics are not clearly marked in the rhythm section parts. The rhythm section must listen at all times to the horns to determine the proper volume to play. Rhythm section volume should be guided by what is happening in the tune. Volume should be adjusted accordingly to complement solos, soli passages, and full tutti "shout" sections.

Rehearsing Jazz Style

The use of scat syllables is an excellent way to achieve proper style and precision both within each section and throughout the entire ensemble. The term "scat syllable" refers to nonsense syllables used by jazz singers when improvising. By saying or singing figures using scat syllables, musical phrases not only become more precise but also adhere more closely to proper jazz style. In rehearsal, first sing or say a phrase applying scat syllables, then play it. Following are some common articulation concepts that apply in most medium to fast swing tunes along with the corresponding scat syllables.

■ Quarter notes should be played "fat" (long and full), but with separation. Use the scat syllable "dot."

■ Two eighth notes tied across a bar line are generally played just like a quarter note—"fat" but with separation. Use the scat syllable "dot."

■ Eighth notes that stand alone should be very short. Use the scat syllable "dit."

■ Eighth-note lines should be approached with a legato tongue or even slurred. The last eighth note in a line of eighth notes should be played short. Use scat syllables "do"-"bah"-"do"-"dit." The articulation style depends somewhat on the tempo of the tune and when it was written. The faster the tempo, the more legato and evenly the eighth notes should be played. Older style swing tunes often call for shorter, more separated eighth notes (more tongue).

       Getting Started with Jazz Band

do bah do dit

■ Quarter notes that are marked long, as well as note values greater than a quarter note should be played with no separation.

dah   dah

■ Following are examples of some common swing figures with scat syllables:

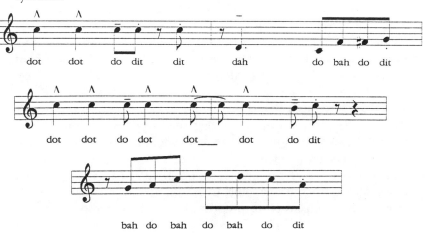

dot   dot   do dit   dit   dah   do bah do dit

dot   dot   do dot   dot____   dot   do dit

bah do bah   do bah   do   dit

■ Occasionally the instruments in the rhythm section have the same written out swing figures as the horn ensemble. It is very important as a member of the rhythm section to recognize when a passage is with the horns and to articulate as if playing a horn. Scat syllables should be applied to these written out rhythm section figures.

When playing a ballad, articulation should be approached more like it would be in concert band music. Most notes are long, and phrases are generally legato. There are fewer situations where stopping the note with the tongue is appropriate. Releases become more critical at slow tempos, so it is important to determine as an ensemble exactly when a note should be released. Also, determine if the end of the note should taper or slightly crescendo to a release. In ballads containing sections that should be interpreted in swing style—the swing articulation guideline should be applied, remembering that a "fat" quarter note at a slow tempo will be much longer than at a fast tempo.

It is very important for students to mark articulation and exact counts of releases in the music in pencil. A good shorthand used by professionals is as follows: A release on four should be marked -4; a release on the and of 2 should be marked 2+; articulation should be indicated by a ^ or – over a note.

Sectionals

It is virtually impossible to have an excellent jazz band without sectional work. Schedule sectionals either one day a week in class, or once a week before or after school if your band meets on an extracurricular basis. Each section has unique problems that can be much more effectively solved in this setting.

Student section leaders should be expected to run these sectionals with your help and guidance. Obviously, some sections will work better on their own than others. It is often most difficult to rely on student leadership in the rhythm section, as there are four different instruments, and most likely no one student will have the knowledge to help the entire section.

Provide students with recorded examples to listen to as a model for style and expression. Give them suggestions for working on difficult technical passages. Give specific instructions about what you expect to be accomplished in each sectional and hold students accountable. You may want to grade individuals on a particular passage of the music during the sectional time. Check on each section frequently to monitor behavior, listen to progress, and make suggestions. It may take some time for students to learn to work in this manner, but you will find that teaching them the skills needed to work effectively together will pay off in the long run. You will find that the students feel more ownership of the band if they have the responsibility to work together in small groups, making musical judgments and solving problems, than if all of the rehearsing is done in full band where you make the creative musical decisions.

Chapter 5

Teaching Improvisation

Teaching jazz improvisation can be very intimidating, especially to the young band director who has little or no background in this area. For a variety of reasons, even many experienced band directors shy away from teaching students to improvise. Many feel it takes too much time or that their students aren't ready to learn. Some even adhere to the age-old myth that the ability to improvise is a gift, not something that can be taught.

The essence of jazz is its *improvisatory* nature. Ignoring this vital aspect of jazz education shortchanges you and your students. One of the most rewarding aspects of teaching is helping students develop the skills necessary to create and express themselves musically. Think of jazz improvisation as musical communication. You would not ask a student to make a speech without proper preparation on the topic to be addressed, yet students are often told to "just play whatever you want" when faced with an improvised solo in jazz band.

Jazz improvisation *can* be taught. Some students will be more successful than others for a variety of reasons including musical aptitude, environment, motivation, technical skill, creativity, knowledge of music theory, aural perception, imitative ability, and practice. It is important to create an atmosphere where students can learn the skills necessary to begin to improvise and where individual creativity and musical expression are encouraged. Teaching improvisation is fun. The pride and accomplishment felt by the students will be your reward for taking the time to expose them to the creative musical process of jazz improvisation.

There are as many ways to teach jazz improvisation as there are teachers. You must find an approach that is comfortable for you. You may want to use a class improvisation method (see Chapter 3) that is published or put together your own materials. No matter what approach you take, the teaching of improvisation should include written jazz theory, development of aural skills, guided improvisation, learning of standard tunes, familiarization with the history of the art form and artists, and opportunities for small combo playing.

Teaching Jazz Theory

A basic knowledge of chord types, scales, and harmonic function will give your students the background necessary for understanding how to approach an improvised solo when provided with chord changes. Present information in small segments and have students practice identifying chords and scales, spelling chords from the written symbols, writing scales, and matching scales to chords. Figure 5 contains common jazz chord symbols and their construction. Jerry Coker's *Improvising Jazz* will provide you with additional material needed for teaching jazz theory. Give short homework assignments weekly, and if possible make computer software, such as Ars Nova's *Practica Musica*, available for students to practice written theory skills. Test students throughout the semester to ensure that these written skills are acquired and retained. Reinforce students' knowledge of jazz theory by *playing* scales, chords, and jazz patterns on a daily basis. Ask students to work from memory as much as possible.

Aural skills are very important to the jazz improviser. Jazz musicians constantly work to improve their ability to imitate, identify, and transcribe aural information. Spontaneous improvisation depends on the ability to listen and respond to music as it is taking place.

Incorporate aural imitation exercises in your daily warm-up. Have the rhythm section play medium tempo swing time—at first simply have them repeat an F7 chord. Play a four-count musical motive on

FIGURE 5			
Symbol	**Name**	**Scale Degree**	**Example**
M7 or Δ7	major seventh chord	1 - 3 - 5 - 7	
m7 or -7	minor seventh chord	1 - ♭3 - 5 - ♭7	
Ø7 or m7♭5	half diminished seventh chord	1 - ♭3 - ♭5 - ♭7	
°7	diminished seventh chord	1 - ♭3 - ♭5 - ♭♭7	
7	dominant seventh chord	1 - 3 - 5 - ♭7	
M6 or Δ6	major sixth chord	1 - 3 - 5 - 6	
7+5 or +7	augmented seventh chord	1 - 3 - #5 - ♭7	

Getting Started with Jazz Band

the piano or your instrument, and ask the band to imitate it by singing or playing. To begin with, use only the notes of an F blues or F pentatonic scale.

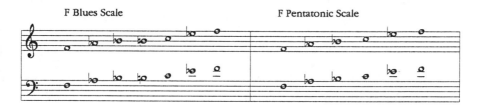

F Blues Scale   F Pentatonic Scale

Always start the motive on the tonic. As the students' skills increase, introduce the chord changes for F blues (figure 6) to the rhythm section and make the musical motives longer and more complex. Always use patterns that are faithful to the jazz language and style. There are many books that contain jazz patterns, or you can create your own. Occasionally call on students to create the motives for class response. Continue to use new sets of chord changes and melodic materials throughout the year. Encourage students to practice in pairs with one student creating ideas and the other imitating what is played. Another good way to practice aural imitation is for the student to sing a four or eight count idea using scat syllables and then attempt to play the idea on his instrument.

FIGURE 6

Basic F Blues

F^7 / / / | $B^{\flat 7}$ / / / | F^7 / / / | F^7 / / / | $B^{\flat 7}$ / / / | $B^{\flat 7}$ / / / |

F^7 / / / | F^7 / / / | C^7 / / / | $B^{\flat 7}$ / / / | F^7 / / / | F^7 / / / :‖

(C^7 / / /) for repeat

Your students should also learn to identify and write down scales, chords, and patterns that they hear. Spend some time in class helping students learn to listen and write down what is heard.

There are excellent ear training tapes available such as David Baker's *Ear Training for the Jazz Musician*. Computer software programs such as *Practica Musica* and *ISIS* include exercises to increase aural skills.

Give short ear-training quizzes occasionally, without grades if you prefer, so that you can monitor progress.

Jazz musicians frequently transcribe recorded solos of the jazz masters. Transcription is an excellent way to improve aural skills while analyzing a particular musician's style and musical ideas. Introduce transcription to your students through a class project. Choose a relatively simple solo of a jazz artist and assign a short passage to each member of the band for transcription. Some of your more advanced students may want to try to transcribe a complete solo as a semester project.

Guided Improvisation

Although it is important to allow students the freedom to improvise without undue criticism, you will need to supply them with some guidelines if their product is to be successful. A good initial approach is to limit the melodic material and concentrate on other musical elements such as rhythm, dynamics, tone quality, and range.

When students are learning a new tune, first have them listen to the chord changes played by the rhythm section. If your rhythm section is not experienced enough to read and play the chord changes at sight, then use an Aebersold recording of the changes at first. After the students are aurally familiar with the chord changes, have everyone play the root of each chord along with the rhythm section or recording. Continue with the other chord tones, and finally create short patterns using scale degrees such as 1–2–1–2 or 1–2–3–1 on each of the chord changes. Be sure that the students understand that the notes in the pattern must match the chord. For example:

- C7 play 1–2–3–1
- Cm7 play 1–2–♭3–1

After the students are comfortable playing chord tones and patterns along with the chord changes, call on individuals to attempt improvised solos. Limit the melodic material to the chord tones and patterns that have been introduced. It is important for every student to feel comfortable attempting a solo. Encourage each student to try to solo, even if only the root of each chord is played with some rhythmic or dynamic variation.

Guide students' selection of melodic and rhythmic material so that their solos make musical sense and are stylistically convincing. Discuss melodic and rhythmic development and encourage students to select a musical idea and work with it. Often, young players try to include too many ideas in one solo. Teach your students compositional devices such as repetition, variation, the use of tension and release, melodic contour, rhythmic augmentation and diminution, and help them shape their ideas into musical communication.

Learning the Jazz Language

In order to communicate effectively through jazz improvisation, a student must become familiar with the art form, the artists and the body of material that constitutes the history and tradition of jazz. This can be accomplished through intensive listening and by playing and memorizing tunes.

Jazz is essentially an aural art; the printed page can only approximate the character and feel of the music. Rehearsal time spent listening is not wasted—structured listening is the best possible way to introduce students to the language of jazz. Spend at least five minutes of every rehearsal listening to jazz, and follow the listening time with specific questions about what was heard. Select big band and combo tunes of various artists and styles for listening. (See Chapter 8 for suggestions.) Question students about instrumentation, style, form, improvisational techniques, and emotional response to the music.

In addition to intensive listening, memorization of standard jazz tunes will help students become familiar with the language. Many of these tunes are published in the Aebersold play-along volumes. Standard jazz tunes are also available in many "fake" books. Even though almost any tune can be found in printed form, it is a good idea for students to try to learn tunes by ear. Remember that jazz is an aural art, and the expressive elements of the jazz language cannot be notated on the printed page. Learning a tune by ear from a recording of a great jazz musician provides the student with a model that incorporates all of the intricacies that cannot be communicated by the printed page. In addition to learning the melody, students can attempt to imitate the tone quality, style, time feel, and expression of the artist.

Incorporating Improvisation Instruction into the Rehearsal

Having examined the individual components that contribute to teaching improvisation, here are some practical suggestions for incorporating an improvisational unit into the jazz band rehearsal. This unit might take six to eight weeks to complete, depending on how often your band rehearses and how much time you choose to devote to teaching improvisation. Your initial goal might be to thoroughly examine one tune a semester.

First select a tune to use for improvisational purposes that meets the following criteria:

- There is an excellent professional combo recording available.
- It is published on an Aebersold play-along volume.
- A good big band arrangement is available that is in the correct key.
- It has relatively simple chord changes.

Some suggested tunes are *The Preacher, Blue Bossa, Now Is The Time, Watermelon Man, St. Thomas, Maiden Voyage, Cantaloupe Island, Work Song, Killer Joe, Blues Minor, Mr. P.C.*, and *All Blues*.

Listen to a professional recording of the tune as an introduction to the unit. Discuss form, style, instrumentation, improvisation techniques, and expressive elements. Also talk about the role of the rhythm section, the communication that takes place among the members of the rhythm section, and the interaction between the rhythm section and the soloists. If possible, provide each student with a tape of the tune for their own practice and study. Have students attempt to learn the tune by ear from the recording.

Next introduce the printed version of the tune with chord changes. Spend time discussing the note content of the various chords. Students must understand each of the chord symbols and be able to write out and play the chords. Ask students to memorize the melody (also called the "head" of the tune) and the chord changes.

Now your students are ready to begin improvising. Follow the procedure outlined in the section on guided improvisation to get them started. You may want to ask students to write out some melodic ideas or motives that can be explored during improvisation. Allow some time for free improvisation, experimentation, or brainstorming. It is helpful to make a clear division between times when students' use of materials is limited and times when anything is acceptable.

One of the most difficult aspects of teaching improvisation is maintaining a balance between creative freedom and the discipline required to achieve a quality product. Ask students to evaluate recorded solos as well as their own improvisations. Discuss what makes a particular solo successful. Explore the question of when an idea is creative and when it is simply gibberish. Work with students to refine musical ideas so that meaning is conveyed, rather than allowing them to play random notes.

Encourage students to practice improvising outside of class. The Aebersold play-along volumes are a great way for students to practice with a recorded rhythm section. Two computer software packages for jazz improvisation, *MiBac* and *Band In A Box,* are excellent if a computer, MIDI, and keyboard setup is available for students' use. With these programs, chord changes for any tune can be entered into the computer, and through MIDI and a keyboard a simulated jazz rhythm section will generate the changes in any key and at any tempo and style. With a little more difficulty, any basic MIDI "sequencer" program can also be used to prepare accompaniments.

As the students are learning to improvise on the tune you have selected, begin rehearsing the full jazz band arrangement of the same tune. When it is time for a public performance, this tune can be programmed with several students ready to play convincing jazz solos. A jazz band arrangement does not have to be performed exactly as written. Use good musical judgment to tailor the arrangement to your band. You can "open up" the solo section of any tune for multiple soloists, and it is acceptable to substitute one instrument in place of another in a solo section of a jazz band arrangement. Be sure that you give each soloist at least one full chorus of the tune. For example, do not divide a 32-bar tune between two soloists. Also, analyze the arrangement carefully so that the *complete* form of the tune is used for each soloist. Occasionally, multiple soloists will engage in "trading fours," a procedure in which the soloists alternate every four measures. The form of the tune remains unchanged. Use written band background parts only when desired.

Combo Playing

One of the best ways for students to develop as jazz soloists is by participating in a combo. Help your more advanced students organize jazz combos made up of a rhythm section and three or four horns, and allow them to perform occasionally on a concert. You need not purchase special arrangements, as part of the experience of combo playing should include working out arrangements. By listening to combo recordings of jazz artists, students can plan an introduction and conclusion to the tune, determine who will improvise, make up background figures, and even harmonize the tune.

Chapter 6

Tips for Successful Performances

Where and When Will Your Band Perform?

Several factors should be considered when scheduling performances for your jazz band. Performances should be a natural outcome of the learning that has taken place. Keep in mind that the band is a school ensemble, not a professional band. The musical growth of the students in the band should be the number one priority. Service, both to the school and to the community, should certainly be a function of the jazz band, but should not become the reason for its existence. Contests and festivals can be valuable motivational and educational experiences for your students, but again should not become the primary focus of the jazz band program.

A reasonable performance schedule might include three to six concerts each semester. The number of performances should be determined by the amount of rehearsal time available, the experience of the band, and the students' availability. Other music department activities should also be taken into consideration. You must evaluate your particular situation to determine an appropriate schedule. Public performances provide incentive to perfect the music, and students' efforts are rewarded with appreciation from parents, teachers, and friends. Too many performances, however, can overload students, interfering with academic achievement and causing them to tire of the jazz band.

Try to schedule a variety of performances such as school concerts, performances for community groups, and participation in jazz festivals. If you are seeking opportunities for your band to perform, contact community groups such as the Lions Club or Jaycees. Retirement communities and nursing homes often welcome school performing groups. In addition to or in place of the traditional school concert, you might try having a "cabaret" with the jazz band performing in the foyer or cafeteria while refreshments are served. This informal atmosphere provides an outlet for jazz combos—consisting of your more advanced students—to perform.

You will find that there are many opportunities to take your band to jazz contests and festivals. Competition can be a positive experience for your students if approached with the correct attitude. Look for festivals that emphasize jazz education. Many offer outstanding clinics that will inform and motivate your students.

Physical Setup

Regardless of where you are performing, you should attempt to duplicate the physical setup that is used in rehearsal. With the saxes seated and the trombones standing, the trumpet section must be elevated to achieve proper balance. Two 8-inch by 4-inch by 16-inch stage tables are ideal to elevate the trumpet section. If it is not possible to elevate the trumpets, then the trombones should sit.

Just as in rehearsal, the rhythm section should be as close to the horns as possible, and the members of the rhythm section should be able to see and hear one another. The correct setup is critical to a successful performance. Frequently, jazz bands seem to set up in a haphazard fashion, which negatively affects their performance. If your band must set up quickly, assign students specific responsibilities to ensure that the process is organized and efficient. If you are in a situation such as a jazz festival where a time limit is placed on your performance, consider set-up time when planning your program. Always check the setup carefully before beginning your performance.

Experiment with musical instrument amplifier settings to achieve the desired results. Each performance location may require different settings. For example, your bass amplifier may be very loud in your rehearsal room, requiring that you keep it set at a low level with a lot of treble in the mix. When you go into your auditorium, it may not be heard at all at that volume and mix. When you rehearse in your auditorium, take time to sit in the audience while your players experiment with the amplifier settings for the guitar, bass, and keyboard. Work with them to achieve the proper tone quality and volume.

Sound Systems

You may want to consider amplifying some or all of the instruments in your band when performing. Although the professional bands in the big band era such as Count Basie, Benny Goodman, and Duke Ellington certainly performed without amplification, there are times when amplification or sound reinforcement is justified. The rock- and funk-style music frequently played by contemporary jazz bands uses prominent electric bass, guitar, and keyboards. It is often difficult for soloists and reeds to compete with the sound level of these amplified instruments. It also may be necessary to use sound reinforcement when performing in a large concert hall or outdoors.

Although sound reinforcement can be very complex, the following suggestions should help you with most of your performance needs. First you must determine if amplification is needed at all. Some performances can be done very effectively without sound equipment, particularly in small or acoustically live rooms or when your band is providing background music during a reception or dinner.

Should you decide that some amplification is needed, you may want to consider using microphones for the soloists and for the acoustic piano only. If you are playing in a concert hall that seats three hundred or less, this configuration should work very well. In a hall of three hundred to one thousand, you may also want to "mike" your reeds, particularly if there are any passages in the music where the saxophones double on flute or clarinet. In a hall that seats more than one thousand, or outdoors, sound reinforcement should probably be used for the entire band.

The acoustics of the performance venue should also be considered. In a room or concert hall that is very "live," less amplification will be needed. You must sit where the audience will be seated and let your ears be the judge. Remember that amplification will not make your band sound better—it will help balance the ensemble, allowing soloists, reeds, and the acoustic piano to be heard more easily. It will also allow the entire band to sound louder and enable them to fill up a larger concert space. You should always strive for the most natural sound possible. Ideally, the audience should not realize that amplification is being used.

For most school jazz bands, a small portable sound system will be the most useful. Almost any performance can be done with a total of fifteen microphones—six for the reeds, four for the brass, two for the soloists, two for the acoustic piano, and one vocal or speaking microphone. If your school auditorium seats more than one thousand people it may have a sound system built into the house. If you are investing in a system for the jazz band, you will want one that is both portable and easy to assemble and run. Following is a list of the components that you will need with basic specifications and suggestions for reliable brands. Remember that this is professional level equipment, which differs from the components of a home stereo.

Basic Sound System

- **Mixing Console or Board**—Sixteen to twenty-four channels with phantom power and four auxiliary sends (these boards are made by Peavy, Soundcraft, TAC, Ramsa, Mackie, and Yamaha).
- **Equalizer**— ⅓ octave or "graphic" (such as one by Yamaha, Rane, or Peavy)
- **Amplifiers**—Amplifiers must be capable of properly powering the loudspeakers. You will need two (one for each loudspeaker) 200 to 400 watts depending on the specifications of the loudspeakers (such as those by Crown, Crest, QSE, and Peavy).
- **Loudspeakers**—You will need a minimum of two full-range (or two-way) speakers, one for each side of the stage. (Try the JBL-Sound Reinforcement Series, Peavy-Acoustic Series, Klipsch, Yamaha, and Electro-Voice.)

- **Speaker Stands**—Speaker stands are not absolutely necessary, but they will allow the loudspeakers to be elevated for maximum efficiency.

- **Microphone Snake Cable**—Multicable snake systems are available in any length and up to thirty-two channels. The snake makes it possible to run all of your microphone lines to the mixing console in one large cable. You can use individual microphone cables to connect microphones to the mixing console, but the snake makes the set up of the sound system much faster and easier. The snake will also alleviate problems that are caused by connecting several microphone cables together to reach the mixing console. (Snakes are made by Pro-Co and Whirlwind.)

- **Microphones**—Perhaps the best all-around microphone for amplification of brass or reeds that is also durable and inexpensive is the Shure SM 58. To mike the reeds and soloists you will need eight of these. If you also want to mike the brass, use one mike for every two brass players. A total of fourteen Shure SM 58s should be sufficient for any performance. A great deal of money can be spent on high-quality microphones that will sound great, but they are also delicate and probably are not the best choice for public school use. The acoustic piano should be miked with two Pressure Zone Microphones (PZM) taped to the inside of the piano, one on the high end and one on the low end. Experiment with placement to get the best sound. Crown makes excellent PZMs; Radio Shack also makes a less expensive PZM. Most PZMs require phantom power either from the mixing console or from a battery pack.

- **Cables**—Purchase at least two microphone cables for every mike. You will also need cable to connect your speakers to amplifiers and to connect the equalizer to the amplifier. (Manufacturers include Whirlwind, Rapco, and Soundcraft.)

- **Direct Boxes**—If you want to control the volume and tone quality of the bass, keyboard, and guitar at the mixing console you will need three direct boxes (such as those by Pro-Co and Whirlwind).

- **Microphone Stands**—You will need a microphone stand for each microphone. Be sure that the stands you purchase have heavyweight bases or are tripod design for stability. For the saxophone section and saxophone solo microphone, purchase booms or goosenecks. Use straight microphone stands for the brass and brass solo microphones. (These are made by AKG and Atlas.)

- **Cases and Racks**—A case for your mixing console and racks (or permanent housing) for your amplifiers and equalizer are a very important part of the sound system. When you travel, the cases will make the system easier to transport, and they will protect the valuable equipment from damage. (Good cases are made by Anvil and ATA.)

Getting Started with Jazz Band

- **Headphones**—a set of headphones will be necessary to listen to each of the channels through the mixing board. (Among the manufacturers are Sony and AKG.)

The system outlined above is very versatile. Additional equipment can be added as needs arise and the budget allows. There are also some extras that you may add as you learn more about sound equipment and assess your particular needs:

- A monitor system
- Microphones for the drum set
- An effects board
- Higher quality microphones

Operating the Sound System

Once you have all of the necessary equipment, you must find qualified people to operate it. Your school may have a student technical crew that operates sound and lighting equipment in the auditorium. Often there is a faculty sponsor or a technical director for the auditorium. Check these avenues for qualified students who would like to work with the jazz band as sound engineers. Select three or four students who you can train to set up, operate, and maintain the sound equipment.

You will want someone operating the mixing board who is familiar with jazz music and who has a concept of the sound of a big band. Your sound engineer should attend some of your rehearsals to learn the music that you are performing. Particular attention should be paid to solos, special amplification problems, and the natural sound of the ensemble.

An excellent book that will provide you with further information about sound reinforcement is *Yamaha Sound Reinforcement Handbook,* by Gary Davis and Ralph Jones. It is written in a practical fashion for the novice. The most important thing is not to be intimidated by the equipment. Use your ears and make musical decisions based on what you want to hear.

Traveling with the Jazz Band

Not all of your jazz band performances will take place in your school, so you must be prepared to travel with the band to perform for community functions, contests, and jazz festivals. Here are some tips that should make your performances on the road easier and more enjoyable:

- Pack all of the band members' music folders in a folio box organized in score order. Assign a band member without a great deal of personal equipment to be responsible for the music box.

■ Always take your own electronic tuner. You know that it is reliable, and both you and your students are familiar with how it operates. Calibrate your tuner to the piano that will be used for your performance. At a contest or festival, simply slip out on stage between performances to calibrate the tuner to the performance piano.

■ Always carry a power strip, at least two extension cords and a two prong to three prong converter.

■ Pack a carpet for your drum set.

■ Pack extra patch cords for the guitar, bass, and keyboards, as these tend to wear out easily.

■ Check in advance to see if there will be risers or stage tables to elevate the trumpets. If not, plan to seat the trombone section or bring portable crates.

■ Give students specific assignments for loading and setting up equipment.

■ When performing in an unfamiliar hall with no rehearsal time, try to listen to other groups that perform before your band to assess the acoustics of the hall. Note in particular the volume and tone quality of the amplified instruments.

■ If amplification is provided by the house system, be sure to communicate your needs clearly to the sound engineer. If you do not like what you hear in your rehearsal or when listening to other groups, ask that changes be made for your performance.

Chapter 7

Parting
Thoughts

As a band director, you are a part of a very exciting and rewarding profession. You are in a position to make a great impact on students' lives. Through involvement in a band program, young people can learn to perform, appreciate, and create music. They are a part of something very special that will be with them for the rest of their lives. You have a responsibility to develop a band program that makes the musical growth of the student the top priority.

"Build it and they will come"—the message of the movie *Field of Dreams*—tells us to focus on our vision and work steadfastly toward its realization. Apply this message to your band program by building a sound student-centered program through excellence in teaching, and the results will be astounding. Parental and administrative support, strong relationships with students, musical excellence, success in competition, and great personal rewards will follow. Certainly the details of everyday tasks must be attended to, but don't allow yourself to be buried in mundane details or to be discouraged by temporary setbacks. Never lose sight of your vision for your program.

A very important part of achieving excellence as a music educator is your own professional growth. If you continue to learn, you will be able to bring fresh ideas to your students. Even though your daily responsibilities keep you very busy, it is important to devote time to your own growth as a musician and educator. Here are some suggestions:

- Join national professional organizations such as the Music Educators National Conference and the International Association of Jazz Educators. These organizations publish professional journals that will keep you abreast of the latest materials and techniques. They also hold regional and national conferences that are rich in opportunities for professional growth.
- Become active in at least one state music organization by serving as a committee member or officer. The contacts that you make with others in the profession are invaluable.
- Take your jazz band to at least one educational jazz festival every year. Attend as many of the clinics as possible. Require your students to attend the festival clinics and spend time in class discussing what was learned.
- Identify areas of your teaching that you feel need improvement and attend summer workshops that address those weaknesses.
- Bring guest artists and clinicians into your school to work with your band and to give you feedback on your teaching.
- Subscribe to jazz magazines such as *Downbeat* and *Jazziz*.
- Spend time listening to all styles of jazz.

Chapter 8

Basic Jazz Library for the Music Educator

Coker, Jerry *Improvising Jazz* and *Listening to Jazz*

Gridley, Mark *Jazz Styles*

Haerle, Dan *Jazz/Rock Voicings for the Contemporary Keyboard Player*

Houghton, Steve *A Guide for the Modern Jazz Rhythm Section*

Simon, George T. *The Big Bands*

Jazz

Resources

Sources for Purchasing Jazz Materials and Equipment

Jazz band music from the major music publishers such as William Allen, Barnhouse, CPP/Belwin, Jenson, Kjos, Kendor, and Hal Leonard can be purchased through your local music store or the vendor from whom you purchase concert band music. Most of the major publishing companies will send you demonstration tapes and materials upon request.

Following are several invaluable sources for jazz music, materials, and equipment. Catalogs are available upon request.

Jamey Aebersold

P.O. Box 1244C

New Albany, IN 47151-1244

Jazz textbooks, play-along book-and-recording sets, Jazz CDs and tapes, combo charts, and much more

Full Compass

5618 Odana Road

Madison, WI 53719

Sound reinforcement equipment

Pender's Music Co.

314 S. Elm

Denton, Texas 76201

Big band and combo music not available elsewhere, jazz textbooks, jazz recordings

Such Sweet Thunder

P.O. Box 1892 Ansonis Station

New York, NY 10023

Authentic transcriptions of jazz classics of Duke Ellington and Count Basie

UNC Jazz Press

University of Northern Colorado

Greeley, CO 80639

Music for young band to very advanced, small combo and big band, vocal charts

Walrus Music Publishing
P.O. Box 11267
Glendale, CA 91226-7267
Excellent selection of medium to difficult charts, professional big band recordings, jazz textbooks, jazz videos, and computer software and hardware

Suggestions for Listening by Instrument

Alto Saxophone—Cannonball Adderley, Ornette Coleman, Eric Dolphy, Lee Konitz, Jackie McLean, Charlie Parker, Art Pepper, Bud Shank

Tenor Saxophone—Gene Ammons, John Coltrane, Stan Getz, Dexter Gordon, Coleman Hawkins, Harold Land, Sonny Rollins, Wayne Shorter, Zoot Sims, Ben Webster, Lester Young

Baritone Saxophone—Pepper Adams, Harry Carney, Serbe Chaloff, Gerry Mulligan

Trumpet—Chet Baker, Terrance Blanchard, Clifford Brown, Miles Davis, Kenny Dorham, Roy Eldridge, Dizzy Gillespie, Freddie Hubbard, Lee Morgan, Fats Navarro, Woody Shaw, Clark Terry

Trombone—Carl Fontana, Curtis Fuller, J. J. Johnson, Frank Rosolino, Bill Watrous, Phil Wilson

Piano—Chick Corea, Bill Evans, Tommy Flannigan, Herbie Hancock, Ahmad Jamal, Thelonious Monk, Oscar Peterson, Bud Powell, Horace Silver, Art Tatum, McCoy Tyner, Joe Zawinul

Bass—Ray Brown, Ron Carter, Paul Chambers, Stanley Clarke, Eddie Gomez, Percy Heath, Charles Mingus, Oscar Pettiford, Rufus Reid

Drums—Louis Bellson, Art Blakey, Kenny Clarke, Elvin Jones, Philly Joe Jones, Buddy Rich, Max Roach, Grady Tate, Tony Williams

Guitar—George Benson, Kenny Burrell, Charlie Christian, Larry Coryell, Barney Kessel, Wes Montgomery, Joe Pass, Jimmy Raney, Django Reinhardt

Vibes—Gary Burton, Terry Gibbs, Lionel Hampton, Milt Jackson, Red Norvo, Cal Tjader

Organ—Jack McDuff, Jimmy Smith, Larry Young

Big Bands—Toshiko Akiyoshi, Count Basie, Louis Bellson, Matt Catingub, Dallas Jazz Orchestra, Duke Ellington, Don Ellis, Gil Evans, Lou Fischer, Bob Florence, Woody Herman, Bill Holman, Thad Jones-Mel Lewis, Stan Kenton, Tom Kubis, Rob McConnell

Violin—Jerry Goodman, Stephan Grappelli, Ray Nance, Stuffy Smith, Joe Venuti, Michael White

Vocalists—Ray Charles, June Christy, Rosemary Clooney, Nat King Cole, Billy Eckstine, Ella Fitzgerald, Billie Holiday, Carmen McCrae, Anita O'Day, Lou Rawls, Frank Sinatra, Mel Torme, Sarah Vaughan, Joe Williams

Acknowledgments

The contributions of the following people helped make this publication possible:

Nicholas Brightman, Applied Music Coordinator and Saxophone Instructor, Purdue University

Kurt Gartner, Assistant Professor of Bands and Percussion, Purdue University

Raul Gonzalez, Sound Engineer, Purdue University

Philip G. May, Trumpet Instructor, Lafayette, Indiana

Joseph Manfredo, Associate Professor of Bands, Purdue University

Nick Schnieder, Bass Instructor, Chicago, Illinois

Glenn C. Williams, Director of Bands, Highland Park High School, Highland Park, Illinois

MENC's
Getting Started
Series

Each book in this series provides an outline to help new teachers, or teachers beginning new positions, gain confidence as they get started.

Getting Started with High School Band. By David S. Zerull. 1994. 52 pages. Stock #1627. ISBN 1-56545-045-0.

Getting Started with High School Choir. By Steven K. Michelson. 1994. 64 pages. Stock #1628. ISBN 1-56545-046-9.

Getting Started with Jazz Band. By Lissa A. Fleming. 1994. 64 pages. Stock #1626. ISBN 1-56545-035-3.

Getting Started with Jazz/Show Choir. Edited by Russell L. Robinson. 1994. 52 pages. Stock #1630. ISBN 1-56545-044-2.

Getting Started with Middle Level Band. By David G. Reul. 1994. 80 pages. Stock #1631. ISBN 1-56545-049-3.

Getting Started with Elementary-Level Band. By Marjorie R. Lehr. 1998. 56 pages. Stock # 1636. ISBN 1-56545-110-4.

Getting Started with Middle-Level Choir. By Patrick K. Freer. 1998. 72 pages. Stock # 1637. ISBN 1-56545-113-9.

Getting Started with Strolling Strings. By Robert Gillespie, with Beth Gilbert and Mary Lou Jones. 1995. 26 pages. Stock # 1632. ISBN 1-56545-079-5.

For more information on these and other MENC publications, write to:
MENC Publication Sales
1806 Robert Fulton Drive
Reston, VA 20191-4348
Credit card holders may call 1-800-828-0229

1626-1.5M-1/99